The Lonely Road

CHAS WILLIAMSON
South Mountain Stories of Devotion

Copyright © 2023 Chas Williamson

All Rights Reserved

Print ISBN: 978-1-64649-331-9

eBook ISBN: 978-1-64649-332-6

Year of the Book
135 Glen Avenue
Glen Rock, PA 17327

This is a work of fiction. Names, characters, businesses, places, events and incidents are either the products of the author's imagination or used in a fictitious manner. Any resemblance to actual persons, living or dead, or actual events is purely coincidental.

Chapter One

The Fruit Man

Elise Showers knocked on the door to Beth Warren's shop. The charming, log-cabin like structure sat along the main highway that ran between Chambersburg and Gettysburg. Even from the outside, the delicious scent of pickling spices made Elise's mouth water.

Beth swung the wide, glass door open. "Morning, Elise. Remind me to give you a key and explain how the alarm system works before you go home this evening. Today, we're canning pickles and then chow-chow."

Elise's friend, and now boss, pointed to a table in the kitchen area. The counters and work surfaces were stainless steel. A six-burner stove was situated next to a double sink. The high table and barstools were the only wooden fixtures in the food preparation area.

"I made cinnamon rolls," Beth continued. "They're your favorites, if I remember correctly.

Help yourself to the Keurig. There's coffee, tea and hot chocolate pods."

Elise slid her purse under the counter and headed for the coffee pot. "Want me to make you a cup?"

"Yes, please. May I have a Kahlua with some hazelnut creamer?" Beth returned to filling jars with sliced cucumbers.

Elise now knew what the plan was for the day. As she prepared the coffee, she felt grateful Beth had hired her. Actually, this was Elise's first job. She wasn't comfortable when there were lots of people around. Beth had reassured Elise, stating if she felt uncomfortable, she could always hang out in the kitchen for a while.

Just as they had for the past two days, the pair spent the morning canning vegetables. Beth was building up her inventory for the upcoming grand opening. After the last jar cooled, the pair wiped off the containers and applied the specialized labels Beth had created.

Elise admired the stickers. "South Mountain Preserves, what a cool name for your business."

"My husband and I came up with that," Beth quipped with a smile.

The pair talked as they worked.

Beth knew Elise's history and asked, "How are things going?"

"With the help of the therapist, I'm coming to grips with my childhood." Elise had been abducted when she was six. "It's hard to imagine. All those years, I believed those two were my parents."

"I'm still amazed you ended up buying a house next to your birth parents' orchard, without even knowing who they were."

Elise nodded. "Even more unbelievable was that my real brother AJ bought the orchard back."

"What drew you here?"

She stopped to consider the question. "I don't really know, but I'm glad I did. And that day, when I stopped over at AJ's and walked into the Summer House... it started coming back to me. All my life, I'd dreamed about playing in that exact building with a red-headed boy named Alex. I didn't even consider that the man living next door might be him. Then, when AJ asked if my name was Elise instead of Laura, it was like somebody threw a switch and the memories flooded my mind."

"It's amazing how God works in our lives, isn't it?"

"I don't know. Do you think—"

A loud rap on the glass door interrupted the conversation. A tall man with wavy, brown hair stood outside.

Elise watched as Beth unlocked and opened the door. The man smiled.

"Hi, my name is Landon White. Last year, I bought a small farm across the road. I have a crop of strawberries that just came in and since I noted the name 'South Mountain Preserves' on the sign out front, I was wondering if you might be interested in buying some of them."

Beth had a large smile on her face. "Hmm, perhaps. Do you have any samples with you?"

"As a matter of fact, I brought some along. Be right back."

While the man returned to his pickup, Beth nudged Elise's arm. "Isn't he cute?"

Elise nodded. "I don't know, but isn't that awfully forward? I mean, just stopping by to see if you were interested?"

"The Lord does work in mysterious ways." Beth laughed.

Elise rolled her eyes. "Sure."

Landon returned with a basket of the red fruit. "Why don't you taste these before we discuss anything."

"Sounds good, let me wash them and I'll get us all some plates." Beth retreated to the far side of the food preparation area.

The man offered a warm smile and his hand. "Hi. Guess you heard me introduce myself. You look familiar. What's your name?"

"Elise Showers. Where did you say you live?"

He pointed to the other side of the highway. "About a mile up the hill. I bought the old Tenderton farm."

Though she'd only moved back to the area three years ago, Elise knew the exact location he was referring to. "I remember the family that lived there when I was little. They had a daughter named Jane. She and I used to play together."

"Have you lived here all your life?"

The thought of those wasted years from when she was told her name was Laura gnawed at her. "No. I grew up in West Virginia, but recently moved back. Perhaps you know my brother, AJ Showers. He has an orchard two roads over from you."

"I've heard of him. Isn't his wife some sort of writer?"

"Um-hmm. He married Terry Faughtinger who writes horror stories."

Landon's face paled. "As in *the* Terry Faughtinger? I love her book *Iverson*, but never dreamed she actually lived in the area."

Before Elise could respond, Beth returned with a tray containing three plates of sliced strawberries, sprinkled with sugar and topped with whipped cream. Three cups of coffee filled out the platter. "Thought we might need something to wash these down. Mind if I offer grace?"

Landon shook his head and Beth offered a brief prayer. It seemed Beth was always talking to the person she called "Lord" or "Father," whoever that was.

The three sat at a small table in the showroom. Beth took a forkful before continuing. "These are very tasty and sweet. So, Landon, tell us about yourself."

"Oh, there's not much to tell. My family had a successful farm in upstate New York. I have two brothers and three sisters. When my parents passed, the farm wasn't enough to support everyone, so we sold it. I used my portion of the inheritance to buy this property. Dad raised beef cattle and my mom grew vegetables. I seemed to have acquired my mother's green thumb, so purchasing this just seemed right."

Elise couldn't help but stare at him. He had large calloused hands, but his expressive, brown eyes were what drew her attention. "Why Pennsylvania?"

"I'm not sure. Something seemed to guide me here."

"Or Someone?" Beth giggled before taking another bite of the fruit.

He laughed, quietly. "Maybe He did. I don't know, but it felt as if I had a connection to the area. As if this was where I was meant to be. With the shorter growing season, staying in New York wasn't the best option. I first looked at Lancaster County, but land prices there are too expensive."

"We used to live there," Beth commented, "but didn't like the congestion from the tourists."

"We? Are you two sisters?"

"No, but Elise and I are close friends. My husband Andy and I bought a place just up the hill." Beth pointed over her shoulder. "We moved here last year, along with my husband's grandparents. They're such nice people."

The man had a smile on his face. "Then I guess we're all neighbors." His eyes fell on Elise. She knew he was assessing her, but not in a creepy way. "If you would like, maybe you could stop by sometime and I'll show you the old place."

"That sounds nice," Beth answered quickly. "Let me talk to Andy about it."

Elise suspected the invitation might have been for her instead. A strange tingling sensation grew in her chest.

Landon looked at her. "What about you, Elise? Maybe you could bring your brother and his wife, the writer. I would like to meet the great Terry Faughtinger."

So that was it. The man really wanted to meet her sister-in-law.

"I'll mention it to them," Elise mumbled. "Perhaps they'll drop by."

Landon's cheeks grew pink. "I hope *you* will visit, even if they're not available."

Hmm, maybe his invitation was for me after all. "Let's see how things go."

"Ahem." Beth cleared her throat. "Can we talk pricing on these berries?"

When Landon turned to face Beth, Elise transported the empty plates to the kitchen area and quickly washed them. After she had dried the dishes, she glanced over and was shocked to see Landon had left.

"Wow, that was quick. Did you decide to buy any?"

Beth nodded. "At that price, I took all he had—ten flats. He has them in the bed of the pickup. I know what we're doing tomorrow." A mischievous smile worked its way onto Beth's face. "Until then, why don't you give the man a hand bringing the crop in while I write his check?"

Elise frowned, but hurried outside to assist. Within minutes, she and Landon had all the fruit on the stainless-steel prep tables in the kitchen area.

The man turned as if to say something, but Beth broke the spell.

"Here you go. I created a bill of sale for my records. Please sign here."

Elise took note of his beautiful signature.

"Guess I'll go now," Landon said. "Perhaps I can come back when my other crops are in season?"

Beth nodded and then shook hands with him. "Looking forward to it."

Landon then faced Elise, offering his hand. She detected a slight tremble when they touched.

"Nice to meet you, Landon."

He bowed slightly as he squeezed her hand. "The pleasure was all mine. Please think about stopping by sometime. Have a day great... uh, I mean a great day." His face flushed just before he turned and walked through the door.

Both ladies watched until he'd climbed in his truck and departed.

Beth broke the silence. "He's a nice man, don't you think?"

Elise did, but wasn't going to admit it. "You never can tell."

Playfully pushing her shoulder, Beth teased. "And in case you couldn't tell... he likes you."

Elise turned to face Beth. "Do you really think so?"

After laughing, her friend patted her hand. "That's my opinion, but I guess time will tell."

Chapter Two

A Song in the Pines

It was still dark when Elise stepped outside. Off to the east, the horizon was beginning to color. This was the time of day she loved best. Adjusting her earbuds so they fit comfortably, a classic Glen Campbell tune kept Elise company as she set out for her morning walk.

While some chose paved roads, Elise loved to hike in the deep woods. The scent of the forest and the texture of the carpet of fallen leaves giving way beneath her feet filled her senses. Today, she trekked along a portion of the Conewago Creek. The waterway just happened to flow along the lowland adjoining the farm where Landon White lived. If she was lucky, maybe she could catch a glimpse of the man she'd met the previous day.

A bend in the stream led her through a grove of white pines. The fragrance of the trees reminded her of the mountain she'd grown up on in West Virginia.

One of her few fond childhood memories, the forest had been her place of solace.

She wasn't quite out of the stand of conifers when a rapid motion to her right drew her attention. Crouching down and removing her earbuds, she watched as seven deer ran past. A shiver crossed Elise's shoulders. With the noise she was making, they should have run the other direction. Something had spooked the animals. And whatever it was, it was somewhere behind her.

Elise focused her attention on the path she'd already walked. It was faint, but she picked up the sound of movement. Whatever was back there must be big and clumsy. Could it be a bear? The local television station had reported one had been seen in the area. Try as she might, she couldn't identify what was making the ruckus.

Quickly stripping the cord from the phone's lightning connector on her cell, Elise selected a different station on her app. She pulled up a loud rock selection that her brother referred to as 'head-banging' music. Moving the volume to maximum, she silenced the station. Elise waited in the early morning dusk for whatever was behind her to appear. If it was a bear, she'd turn on the music and hopefully, the sudden loud noise would scare it away.

The darkness of the early morning hampered her vision. The unseen thing back there drew closer, but had slowed. Suddenly, a strange sound filled the air, softly at first, but with increasing volume. She wasn't one hundred percent certain, but it seemed someone was singing (or trying to).

"Oh, what a beautiful morning..."

Elise snuggled closer to the trunk of the tree. It was a man's voice and the closer he came, the sweeter his voice sounded. The male changed the direction of his travel path from the west side of the copse of trees to the east. Elise crawled to her left to avoid detection. Because of the low-hanging boughs of the pines, his face was hidden behind the needles as he passed just thirty feet away.

Her unseen morning companion now walked slowly along the stream bed, but continued to sing songs from the musical *Oklahoma*.

His figure had almost faded away when she saw him descend the bank toward the flowing water. Elise knew there was a small waterfall across the creek in that approximate location. Only the top of his head was visible as the man bounced across the stream, most likely by jumping on the stones along the fall.

As she observed, he climbed the other grade and headed directly east. The sun suddenly crested the horizon. Just beyond the edge of the forest, a glimmer caught her eye. Though too far away, she supposed it was the reflection of the sun on the dewy spider webs that hung from the metal fence. The barrier surrounded Landon's pasture.

Elise briefly lost sight of the other person, but when he popped out of the trees, the male again came into view. He suddenly stopped singing, turned and appeared to look in her direction. He was silent for almost a minute. Then, the solitude of the early day was split by a different song, this one coming from another Rogers and Hammerstein musical—*South Pacific.* "*Some enchanted evening.*" His words slowed, but filled her with a vision of hiding behind a curtain being at a party, watching everyone else... until she realized someone was smiling at her.

Again, he appeared to look directly to where Elise was hidden amongst the pines. Just before the male turned away, he raised his hand as if to bid her farewell. Within seconds, he jumped the fence and continued his trek.

She turned and sat back against the trunk of the tree. She realized she was breathing erratically. Elise was sure the man had been Landon White, but had he seen her? And if he did, were his songs random, or were the words intended as a message for her?

***

Landon wiped his brow after sliding the last box of peas into the bed of the truck. He wanted to shower before stopping over at Beth's shop. Hopefully the lady would purchase some or all of his crop.

But that wasn't what he was looking forward to the most. Instead, it was the anticipation of running into Elise. He had recognized her face when they met. She was the woman he'd often observed walking through the woods behind his pasture.

Stopping on the porch, he watched as a bee flew from flower to flower. He loved the flying insects for two reasons—the sweet honey they produced, and the fact that they pollinated his crops.

Standing there, a face materialized in the flowers. The image belonged to Elise. After their introduction, he had googled her name and was astounded by his search. The poor girl had been abducted when she was six. Her kidnappers hypnotized Elise and created alternate childhood memories, with them as her parents. After the pair died fifteen years later, she returned to Pennsylvania. Unknowingly, she'd bought a house right next to where her real parents had lived. Just a little over two years ago, Elise discovered the truth about who she really was.

He spoke out loud as he showered. "I feel terrible about what happened to her. Must make it really hard to trust anyone after that."

Landon understood if he wanted to build a relationship with her, he'd need to do it carefully. And he wanted to be her friend, and who knew? Maybe something more in time. Why? Because Elise had been on the forefront of his mind since he first noticed her walking in the woods long before Beth Warren introduced them.

Finally finished with his shower, he donned his cleanest 'work' shirt. The thought of Elise's beautiful, brown eyes and enchanting smile filled his heart. Landon didn't know why he was infatuated with Elise, but he most certainly was. He'd even dragged himself out of bed one day last week and took the trail where he had seen her before, hoping to run into her. Of course, he hadn't. Landon knew it was just his imagination, but he'd felt her presence that morning. He'd even pretended she was waiting for him in the trees and had sung to her.

Sliding his pickup onto the road and heading in the direction of the canning shop, Landon laughed as he recollected that day. "I bet I scared the birds away with my awful voice."

With his mind focused on the pretty young lady, his destination appeared quickly. An elderly couple stood outside the shop, talking with Beth and Elise.

Landon noted his own hands were sweaty. He climbed down from the cab and waved. "Morning."

Smiles greeted him, but it was Beth who spoke. "Good morning, Landon. Let me introduce you to my husband's grandparents."

The senior couple was polite, but departed soon after Landon's arrival. He couldn't help but notice how shy Elise was acting today.

Beth turned to face him. "It's really good to see you again. Did you bring more strawberries or," a teasing smile filled the woman's face, "maybe this is a social visit?"

He couldn't help but notice the pink that appeared on Elise's cheeks and how quickly she looked away. His own cheeks were warm as well.

"Uh, my peas are coming in. I have a dozen or so bushels in the bed. I was wondering if you'd be interested."

"I might take one for home, but I'm not sure how well home canned peas would sell here."

Landon tried to hide his disappointment. "Okay."

Beth's expression changed. "Tell you what. I'll buy two more and see if anyone purchases them at my store."

"I'd appreciate that."

"Maybe you could sell them at the market on Saturday." Both Beth and Landon glanced at Elise, who had uttered the words. The girl turned to face her boss. "I know this is our first time there... and you mentioned we don't have all that much to sell. Could we maybe partner with him?"

Beth put her hand to her mouth and seemed to study Elise. The shop owner abruptly focused her attention on Landon. "What other crops do you have ready?"

"Uh, besides peas? Just strawberries, radishes and some lettuce. I also have some individual vegetable plants I grew from seeds."

"Excuse us for a moment." Beth motioned to Elise and the pair walked inside.

Landon whispered to himself. "Oh, no. I hope that didn't get her in trouble with Beth."

Within moments, the pair returned. Elise's face was now scarlet, but a smile graced Beth's face. "Mr. White, I have a proposition for you. I'm willing to split the market space with you on a couple of conditions."

"Such as?"

"First, I get ten percent of your sales."

He shrugged. "That's reasonable."

"Plus, you have to be there, and you'll need to help set up and tear down." She offered her hand. "Deal?"

Smiling, Landon shook with her. "Sounds great to me."

The business owner giggled. "Oh, there is one other thing... I won't be there. It will just be you and Elise."

Chapter Three

Jammed Up in Gettysburg

"That's the last of it." Landon slid the final box of goods into the bed. "Did you eat breakfast this morning?"

Elise's arms tingled as the man held the door for her. "Not yet. I overslept this morning." That wasn't the truth at all. She'd woken in the middle of the night and couldn't get the thought of the market (or maybe it was her stand mate) out of her mind.

He climbed in next to her and offered a warm smile. "Maybe we can stop at the Ragged Edge for a quick bite before we set up?"

"What's that?"

"It's a really cool coffee shop along the York Road."

"I see."

It was quiet in the cab until he spoke again. "Would you like to listen to some music?"

"Okay."

"What do you normally listen to?"

They passed a cemetery on the right and for a brief second, she thought of the people who had pretended to be her parents. The two loners she had buried in the West Virginia hills. The ones who had robbed her of her childhood.

"I'm sure you'll find it boring, but I like the old classic Country stuff the most. Glen Campbell, Buck Owens, George Jones... artists like that. What about you?"

The man began laughing. Was he making a fool of her?

"What's so funny?"

"I have some CDs in the glove box. Open it up."

Elise popped the latch and the door opened. A half dozen compact disc cases were neatly stored inside. Her mouth fell open when she read the title of the one on top—*Glen Campbell, My Hits and Love Songs*. She quickly closed the box and focused her eyes on the road.

There was concern in Landon's voice. "What's wrong?"

"H-how did you know?"

"What do you mean?"

"There's no way they could be yours. How did you find out what kind of songs I liked? You checked into me, didn't you?" Her breath was intermittent. This couldn't be happening.

The man lifted the turn signal and pulled into the lot of a convenience store just next to the airstrip. "What's wrong Elise?"

"This, this is... I don't know. It feels fake. I've had enough of that in my life. Maybe we should turn around."

"Whoa! I apologize. I wasn't trying to upset you. Yes, I did a web search and discovered what happened to you, and I'd wouldn't do anything to make you uncomfortable."

"But the CDs? There's no way..."

"They're mine. I also like classic Country... and '70s love songs... and even numbers from Rogers and Hammerstein. If you take another look at my collection, you'll discover those CDs as well. That's who I am. My dad loved Country while my mom preferred the hippie stuff. And I had a sister who performed in our high school musicals."

Her pulse was returning to normal. "I-I'm sorry. After everything that happened..." Elise's voice trailed off.

Landon touched her arm. "I wasn't trying to upset you. I promise I'll never do that intentionally. Would you like me to take you back to the shop?"

I over-reacted. "No, I just... I had it all wrong, that's all. Let's head to the market. Please forgive me and let's forget this ever happened."

"There's no reason to ask forgiveness. I understand."

Yeah, I bet you do. "Thanks."

"But there is one extremely important thing I do want you to consider at this very moment in time."

A chill ran down her spine. "What's that?"

"What kind of coffee are you going to get?"

***

Despite stopping for a croissant and java, they had plenty of time to set up. The wooden display case for the preserves had been handcrafted in such a way that it could be quickly collapsed for transport. Beth had told Landon that her husband's grandfather had built it for her. It easily fit on the portable table.

"You think this setup looks okay?" Elise had fussed over the display quite a bit.

Landon walked around to face the stand. "I think it looks fabulous."

She shot him a smirk. "I think you're just saying that so you won't upset me."

"Well, when I checked you out on the internet, it did mention never to insult your jar display."

Elise's face paled briefly before returning to normal. "You're picking on me, aren't you?"

"Of course. Friends do that."

She stared at the small table he'd brought. Quart containers of peas and strawberries, pint boxes of red radishes, bags of greens and a few small potted plants haphazardly occupied his part of the stand.

"Do you want me to arrange this stuff or do you like just having it thrown together?"

Inside he was smiling, but he feigned surprise. "What? Didn't I do a good enough job?"

"Not really. It looks like you dumped it all out of a box and said, 'here ya go'."

"Hmm, might you be saying it needs a woman's touch?"

She wrinkled her nose at him. "It might help."

He waved his arm as if offering it to her. "By all means, please do."

Much to Landon's surprise, the way the girl rearranged his wares made the stand much more inviting.

The market opened around nine but the interest was light. A couple of customers stopped by, mainly to sample the jams and jellies. One or two customers bought a few jars. As far as Landon's wares, there appeared to be no interest.

During a slow period, Elise turned to him. "Mind excusing me for a few minutes? I need to find a restroom."

"Sure. I'll hold down the fort."

Landon watched as Elise headed west along the main street in the direction of the coffee shop. She was pretty, but there was something else about her that drew him in.

After the brief misunderstanding on the drive in, Elise had tried to smooth things over by asking about his family and childhood. Of course, he had plenty of funny stories which she enjoyed. The lady's eyes were beautiful when she laughed.

A couple stopped in front of him. They perused the jams before asking for a sample of the strawberry preserves. He donned gloves and spread some of the red jelly on a cracker. The couple asked for other samples. He guessed they were grazers, as Elise referred to the people who only sampled with no intention of buying.

"Excuse me, sir. Is that strawberry jam?"

He looked up to find Elise standing there with two cups of coffee. Landon couldn't help but smile.

"Why yes, ma'am, it is."

"I see... and was it made from the fresh strawberries you have there?"

"Actually, it was."

The pair who were munching on the jam-covered crackers were watching the interaction.

Elise gasped. "Wait, are those berries from the famous Strawberry Fields of White Farms?"

He had no idea where she was going with this, but the reaction of the couple was hilarious. "You are quite perceptive."

"And are those berries the ones I read about, what they referred to as the 'Special, South Mountain Red Reserves'?"

"They are and they're the last of the season."

"Then I'll take all of them, as well as the jams."

The couple exchanged a worried glance and then the woman spoke up.

"Excuse me, but we were here first. *We* will take all of the strawberries and ten jars of the jam."

Elise harumphed and commented, "The nerve of some people!" She stormed off.

After the couple departed down Baltimore Street, Elise returned and presented Landon with a cup of coffee. "Here you go."

He couldn't help but laugh. "You're a nut. Where'd you come up with that?"

"I don't know. It just popped into my head." She joined him with a giggle. "I'm not sure, but you seem to have some sort of crazy effect on me."

"Really?"

Elise's smile faded and her expression sobered. "Actually, you're starting to."

Chapter Four

A Forecast of Change

As spring turned into summer, Elise found herself spending lots of time with Landon. He was a frequent visitor at the shop because he and Beth had formed a sort of alliance for their businesses. The South Mountain Preserve store carried his fresh produce and the two businesses shared stands at several farmers' markets. And of course, Elise was the one who went along with Landon to sell the products she and Beth canned.

But their time together wasn't limited to just work. Sometimes, when the weather was nice, Landon would occasionally join her for morning strolls in the woods. One mid-June day, he met her just down the road from her house. The sun was waiting to christen the morning.

"Morning, Elise."

"Hi there. How are you this morning?"

"I'm well. I was thinking... what are you doing Sunday?"

"I don't know," Elise answered. "Probably hanging out with my brother and his wife. What about you?"

He touched her hand. "I was thinking about maybe taking a drive."

"Where to?"

"Baltimore. Want to come?"

She noticed Landon's hand was still touching hers. "What are you planning on doing?"

"I'm not sure. Maybe see the Inner Harbor or... I thought possibly we could do a harbor cruise. Get some hard-shell crabs... stuff like that."

"We?"

"Yes—that is, if you'd come with me?"

"I don't know. I've never been to Baltimore."

"It's totally up to you."

"Let me think about it."

The rest of the walk was pretty routine, although they did find a box turtle in a boggy area of the trail.

Just before their walk ended, she turned to Landon. "Is that offer for a drive on Sunday still valid?"

"Of course."

Her hand covered her mouth as soon as the words escaped it. "Then we've got a date."

***

Elise arrived at work to find Beth peeling yellow plums. A young girl was playing with dolls in the corner of the kitchen area.

"Morning, Beth. Who is this?"

"This is my little sister, Angie. She's staying with Andy and I for a couple of days."

After saying hello to the child, Elise made a cup of coffee and joined Beth in preparing the fruit.

Beth eyed her strangely. "What's up with you today?"

"What do you mean?"

"I don't know, but there's something different about you—sort of a glow."

Feeling her cheeks warm, Elise concentrated on the plums. "I wouldn't know why."

The door to the shop opened. Landon walked until he stood directly in front of Elise. It was a little tough to get her breath to go in.

"Nice to see you, Landon." Beth was the one who had spoken. "Can I help you?"

Why are his cheeks so red?

He held out a pair of earbuds. "I just wanted to bring these, in case you needed them. I think you dropped it this morning, Elise."

"Thanks, but you didn't have to run over with them."

The man lowered his voice to a whisper. "I really wanted to see you one more time before I started my day."

"Okay, thanks."

He looked a little disappointed when he left.

The door was barely closed before Beth started in on her. "This morning? What did you *two* do? Must have been something special to give you that glow."

Now, it wasn't just her cheeks that were warm. "We went for a walk to start our day."

"But you've done that before, haven't you?"
"Well, yes."
"Then what was different?"
"We talked about going for a drive to Baltimore on Sunday."

Her boss set down her paring knife and stared at her. "You two are going on a date?"

"It's, uh, not really, umm... I guess we are. Landon and I are going on a date, as friends, of course."

"I'm happy for you." Beth's expression changed as she watched Elise. "What's wrong?"

Her arms were suddenly shaky. "I've never been on a date before. What should I do?"

"First, let's talk about what you're going to wear."

"I, I don't know. Do I have to wear anything in particular?"

"Maybe a dress."

"I only have one and that's the long, pink gown Teresa and AJ bought me for their wedding. Should I wear that one?"

Beth giggled. "No, that's too formal. We should get a different one. I think it's time we called in the reinforcements."

"What do you mean?"

"Saturday, after the farmers' market, how about if my best friend Selena and I take you shopping?"

"For what? To buy a dress?"

Holding up her hands, Beth had never had such a huge smile. "Oh honey, it's about more than the dress. We're going to have a girl's day out."

Chapter Five

Girl's Day Out

It was late afternoon when Selena parked her orange car in the lot in Paradise. The building in front of them seemed vaguely familiar.

"Wait, I think AJ and Terry brought me here." Elise glanced at Beth. "That was the weekend when AJ proposed to her. You ran the bed and breakfast back then, remember?"

Beth nodded. "I sure do. I had a lot of good times and met some very nice people there." She winked at Elise. "And some oddballs as well."

Selena stepped out of the car. "Ignore Beth. She's referring to me and when I stayed there. Beth neglects to reveal that the two of us were BFFs in high school." The woman shook her head and directed her words at Beth. "I'm surprised the authorities allowed you out into the public without the orange jumpsuit. What, were you on work release?"

Beth made a motion with her forefinger next to her temple, indicating her old friend was crazy. "Selena's a nurse, but I think all that radiation from patient x-rays affected her brain. She lost her lead apron, you know?"

Elise couldn't help but smile. "You two, I swear. I really enjoyed today. I wish I had a best friend to share my life with, like the two of you do."

The bell on the door tinkled when Beth opened it. A beautiful lady sat just inside the door. An expression of joy filled the short blonde's face as she jumped from her stool and hugged first Beth, then Selena and then Beth again. "It's so good to see you. It's lonely without you hanging around."

"I missed you as well, Sophie. It seems like it's been forever."

After a few more words, the lady seated them at a table overlooking the garden. Almost immediately, a server took their orders.

Elise watched the waitress leave. "I think I met the lady with the British accent last time I was here."

Beth smiled. "That's Sophie Miller. She owns this shop and her family lives next door to the B&B. Over the five years I managed the business, Sophie and I grew close."

"It must be special, having a bunch of friends."

After their tea pots had been delivered, Selena spoke. "Beth told me a little bit about you. I'm sorry about what you went through. If you'd like to talk, both of us are great listeners."

After drawing a deep breath, Elise began. "I've never been the type of person to discuss my feelings, but my therapist tells me I should, every chance I can. Here goes. My childhood was very lonely. We lived on top of a mountain, far away from everyone. The people I lived with, I believed they were my mother and father. The woman was a teacher at one time, so she home-schooled me. The man was a lawyer who left every morning and returned at night. If we needed something, he was the one to get it."

Both ladies had somber expressions, but it was Beth who spoke. "Didn't you have friends to play with?"

"No. It was very remote. I thought I was happy because I didn't know any better. They certainly didn't prepare me to face the world."

Selena now queried, "How did you happen to end up in Adams County?"

"I woke up one morning and couldn't find them. When I went into their bedroom, they were both dead. I had no idea what to do, so I ran down the road until I found someone. It was actually our neighbor, Ellen. She called the police and helped me afterwards."

"What happened to your parents?"

"They were *not* my parents. The woman had been sick for a while. And they think when he found her dead, he intentionally overdosed on pills."

Beth rubbed her hand. "I'm sorry."

"Ellen was so surprised to find they had a child after living next to them all those years. She worked hard to help me prepare for a new life, one of freedom. And somehow, on my first long trip taking a drive, I ended up passing the house where I now live. It was for sale, and immediately, I knew that was where I belonged. Ellen helped me buy it."

Selena shook her head. "You never left the place where they kept you?"

"Only once or twice. I remember being bitten by a snake one time and they took me to a hospital. I was so frightened by all the people. The two who raised me had filled my head with how mean and horrible people were. Funny, isn't it?"

Beth responded, "What's that?"

"They drilled into my mind how evil people were, but now I realize—they were the real monsters."

"I'm glad God kept you safe and brought you here. And how He led you to buy the house next to your brother."

Anger suddenly welled up inside of Elise. "I'm sorry, but I am *not* a believer. If there really is a god, why did he allow me to be abducted? To never see my real father and mother alive again? My entire childhood was destroyed."

Beth took her hands. "Bad things happen to good people. I think God allows trials and tribulations to happen to help us grow and teach us. Those things happen so we can reach our full potential."

"Right. And what did taking me away from my real family for all those years teach me?"

"There are certain things we don't understand," Selena contributed. "My mother died when I was four. I struggled with that loss for years. Why was she taken from me? Maybe so I could learn the value of love. To make sure I would never miss the opportunity to tell those who really matter what they mean to me."

Elise pulled her hands from Beth. "If there was such a person as this god you speak of, and he was as all powerful and ever loving as some television preachers proclaim, why would he do this to me?"

"Neither of us has the answer to that," Beth continued. "But He is real. I believe that there's a battle going on between good and evil, one we can't see. And I truly am certain that He delivered you out of that situation. He has a plan for our lives, and yours as well."

"Some plan," Elise scoffed. "Depriving me of my childhood."

Selena's expression was one of compassion. "You know Beth and I are best friends. We were like that in high school, but our friendship faded over time. I lost my mom when I was four, the man I loved when I was eighteen, my father at twenty-two, and the job I adored at twenty-eight. Like you, I could have been bitter. But two years ago, I ended up back in Lancaster for a visit. I happened to stay at the same inn Beth managed. I ended up reconnecting with her and marrying Trey—the man I lost when I finished high school. Out of all the places I could have stayed and people I might have met, it happened that way. So, were they all unbelievable coincidences... or did Someone direct my steps? I believe it was God who planned this."

"That's easy for you to say. You have everything anyone could want."

"Yes, but the path to get to this place and time—that's what made me who I am today."

Beth again took and squeezed Elise's hands tightly. "And your journey, the one that brought you here, with us... it's not over. I have faith that God has something special planned for you."

"Good for you. Can we change the subject?"

"Of course, but please keep an open mind over what Selena and I shared about God."

Elise rolled her eyes. "Sure."

Beth took a sip from her cup. "Are you looking forward to your date tomorrow?"

A chill rolled across Elise's shoulders. "Yes, but I'm scared."

Selena laughed. "That's natural. What concerns you?"

"That maybe I won't look nice for Landon... or might say the wrong thing... or do something incredibly stupid. I shared with you that this is my first date. I'm afraid I'll lose his friendship if I mess up."

Elise caught the wink Beth shot at Selena. "In other words, Elise needs help from her cheering section before the big game."

"She certainly does. What time is Landon picking you up?"

"Seven-thirty. We're going to catch breakfast on the way down."

"Why don't you come over to my place at six? Selena and I will help you get ready."

"Why?"

"Because that's what friends do for each other."

A warmth now took hold of Elise. "Okay, but will you make me one of those cinnamon rolls to hold me over?"

Both the other women were beaming, but Beth was the one who responded. "Absolutely! Your wish is my command."

Chapter Six

A Day to Remember

Landon stepped out of his truck. He took in the beautiful Tudor house that dominated the landscape. It was the first time he'd been to Beth Warren's home. Landon had been confused when Elise texted him to pick her up here.

A tall man greeted him, introduced himself as Beth's husband and then led him up the stairs to the kitchen area. Landon immediately recognized Beth, but hadn't met the other couple sitting at the bar drinking coffee.

Beth's smile was ear to ear. "I poured you a cup of coffee while you wait for Elise. Is that okay?"

"Uh, sure." He took it and sat down. Beth introduced him to the pair—Selena and Trey Brubaker. They were Beth's neighbors.

The gentle conversation quelled his fears and after a while, they all shared a laugh or two while waiting. Suddenly, everyone grew quiet and all eyes focused on something behind him.

Landon turned and felt his jaw drop open. Standing before him was Elise, but he'd never seen her dressed like this. She wore a yellow sundress and a white hat with flowers on the brim. But the thing that amazed him the most was the beauty of her eyes.

"Good morning, Landon."

"Hi, Elise. Wow, do you ever look pretty this morning."

The girl's cheeks blushed. He had a hard time concentrating on the rest of the visit inside the Warrens' home. His every attention was focused on Elise.

Almost before he knew it, they had bid farewell to the group and were in his truck. He struggled for something intelligent to say.

Elise beat him to it. "You're quiet. Is everything okay?"

"It's just, well, you simply look beautiful today. Uh, not meaning you don't look that way every day." He was conscious of how underdressed he was in shorts and a golf shirt. "I wish I would have worn something better."

"You look fine to me. Beth and Selena took me shopping yesterday and helped me get ready this morning." She removed her hat. "Do you like how they did my hair?"

Her long locks had been braided along the top of her head. "I've never seen a prettier sight."

Even though they'd eaten together before, it had always been on work trips. But this morning, everything seemed special. Their conversation over breakfast and during the long drive to the inner harbor felt so natural, even if the topics were about the weather and the sights they passed.

He parked his old truck in a parking garage across from the National Aquarium.

"I've never been in a big city before. Is it dangerous?"

He detected a trembling in her hand when he helped her out of the cab. "It's perfectly safe, and besides, I'm right here with you."

Though he offered his arm, she didn't take it. The girl's eyes were large as she studied the mixed sights of people, traffic and the water.

The inside of the aquarium was packed with people. Elise kept very close to him and did her best to avoid the crowds.

After viewing the dolphin show, Elise whispered, "I need to use the restroom."

Landon led her to it and waited outside the entrance. There was a long line and it was a while before she exited.

Immediately, he sensed something wasn't right. Elise was frantically scanning from side to side, looking for him.

"Hey, you okay?"

An expression of relief filled her face as she ran to him. He noted how she grabbed his arm and tightly held it. "All these people... it's making me nervous. This was fun, but can we do something else now?"

He sensed how foreign it must feel to Elise to be in such an urban area. "Actually, I was about to ask if you wanted to see Baltimore... from the water."

"How would we do that?"

"By taking a cruise."

"I've never been on a boat before. Is it safe?"

"Of course. And I'll be right there beside you."

They boarded a harbor sightseeing ship and found a secluded spot to sit. Landon couldn't help but smile as she clung to him. A warmth started where her hand touched his skin, traveled up his limbs and settled in his heart. During the whole trip, Elise firmly held his hand.

After their return, Landon took her to a seafood restaurant where they ordered hardshell crabs. When the waitress brought out the steaming pile of crustaceans, Elise appeared confused. "How do I eat these?"

Grabbing a wooden hammer and a knife, he explained how to remove the shell. He deposited lumps of backfin and claw meat on her plate. "You have to work for it, but these are a delicacy."

Tentatively, Elise nibbled at the white meat. "Wow. This is really good." Within minutes, the girl finished off the first one and reached for another.

All too soon, the sun dipped behind the tall buildings and it was time to leave. As they navigated out of the city, he couldn't help but notice the joy on Elise's face.

"What did you think of Charm City?"

The dreamy expression in her eyes really answered his question, but he smiled at her words.

"I never imagined a place like this existed or that a date could be so magical. Thank you for taking me here and sharing your day."

"Would you like to go out again?"

"Yes, yes. Where to?" Her words came out excitedly.

"I don't know... maybe DC? We could see the Smithsonians."

"Who are they? Your relatives?"

He bit his tongue to stifle the laughter. "No. The Smithsonians are museums. Would you like visit them?"

There was no hesitation in her response. "Yes. When can we go, tomorrow?"

Landon laughed. "That's Monday and I have a lot to do around the farm. But... how about next Sunday?"

She reached for his hand. "I guess that's okay, but do I have to wait a whole week to see you again?"

Shocked at her response, he almost swerved off the highway. "No. How about a picnic tomorrow night, either at your house or mine?"

"Yes." She was silent for a moment. "Can I ask you something?"

"Absolutely. What is it?"

Elise swallowed hard. "I've never had a best friend before. Will you be mine?"

Chapter Seven

A Roar in the Woods

After the trip to Baltimore, Landon and Elise became inseparable. They took hikes through the woods every morning, rain or shine, and split hosting each other for dinner. One thing Elise knew how to do was cook. No matter what she served, it was delicious.

When the nights were clear, they'd often lay on a blanket and talk about the stars, planets and just about everything else in life. They spent a lot of time discussing God and whether He was real. Landon couldn't help but see the Creator in everything, from the delicacy of a maple leaf to the constellations above. And every Sunday, they explored the outside world together.

Landon had fallen head over heels in love with Elise, but didn't push things. She was slowly opening up to him, sharing what happened during the years she'd been held in captivity. Landon knew the girl really needed a friend, so that's what he was. Despite wanting to kiss Elise and tell her how he felt, he refrained. Landon sensed how fragile she must feel inside. He patiently waited for Elise's feelings to match his.

The Labor Day weekend was approaching. One day, Landon came into Beth's shop to drop off cantaloupes and some of the last of his sweet corn. He'd no sooner stepped through the door when Elise ran over to greet him.

"Landon, guess what?"

Her eyes seemed to glow. Elise was so pretty when she was happy.

"I don't know, what?"

"Beth and Selena are going camping over the holiday. And here's the best part. They invited us to come along."

Beth came out of the kitchen area. She was using a towel to dry her hands. "Morning, neighbor. I was just telling Elise about Knoebels. Have you ever been there?" The lady had that look on her face, the expression that meant she was going to tease him.

"I've heard of it, but no. I've never been there."

"It's an old-time amusement park." Beth went on to describe the setting and attractions. "Selena and I are camping with our husbands. We thought you and Elise might also want to come."

Elise grabbed his arm. "Can we, can we? I've never been there."

Joy seemed ready to explode from Elise.

"Uh, sure," Landon committed. "But we'll have to figure out what kind of supplies we'll need. I don't have a tent."

"You don't need one." Beth laughed. "Ours sleeps ten. And we'll come up with a joint menu so we can cook together. It will be so much fun."

"I'll need to find someone to feed the animals when we're gone."

Elise clapped her hands in excitement. "I'll ask my brother. I'm sure he won't mind." She stood in front of him, so ecstatic. "Can we go, please?"

Landon smiled. "Of course. Anything for my Elise."

***

Turning off Route 487, the road fell away into the hollow. Elise took in the storybook houses and the lumber yard. At the bottom of the hill, Landon turned to follow Beth's red Explorer as it crossed a modern bridge that led to the campground. Slightly downstream was an old wooden covered bridge. As they continued up the hill, the sight of camping units on the right was dwarfed by the tall wooden piers to their left.

She touched Landon's arm. "What is that?"

"It's a roller coaster. They can be frightening, but if you want to, we can ride it."

Elise couldn't imagine anything being scary, not with Landon around to protect her. The man brought a sense of safety and security into her life she'd never experienced before. "Maybe, but let's see."

After stopping at the camp store, they followed the Warrens' SUV to the far side of the campground. Their site was in an area called the 'Canadian Provinces'. It didn't take long to set up.

Elise noted a repetitious far-off rumbling followed by screams. "What's that noise?"

"That's the Phoenix," Beth answered. "It's the best wooden roller coaster in the world."

"Landon said they can be scary. Is that why people are screaming?"

"I think it's because of the sudden drop," Selena replied, with a smile on her face. "Maybe you can ride it with Beth... that is, if you can stand her shrieking. My friend is a wimp when it comes to rides. I mean, she needs Valium before even getting on the Merry-go-round. And we won't even discuss her needs before, or after, the Tilt-A-Whirl."

"Don't listen to her," Beth advised. "The only thing scarier than the Phoenix is driving with Selena." Beth turned to her friend and stuck out her tongue before facing Elise again. "Want to ride the Phoenix with me?"

"No, thanks." Elise shook her head. "I might try it, but I want Landon by my side. I don't think anything will frighten me as long as I'm with him."

Chapter Eight

All Dreams End

Their time in Elysburg couldn't be going any better. Over the last two days, Landon had accompanied Elise on every single ride at the amusement park, except one. He'd saved the skyride for their last night. It had previously been a ski lift in New England, but the staff installed the ride on the side of the mountain that overlooked the park. Beth had secretly suggested he might want to take Elise on that one at sunset.

The three couples spent their Sunday at the Crystal Pool. Elise had never been swimming before. But under Selina's instruction and watchful eye, Elise was soon able to keep her head above water as she splashed around.

In the late afternoon, they headed back to the tent. Within minutes, Trey and Andy had a roaring campfire going. While some of Landon's sweet corn were being steamed, the three men cooked Italian sausages in the flames.

Landon smiled to himself as Elise raved about the food. After dinner and cleanup, he noted the sun was about to set. He walked to where Elise sat in a lawn chair.

"Hey kiddo, want to take a walk?"

"Sure. Are we all going?"

"I was hoping we could go alone this time. If you don't mind. There's something special I want to share with you."

Her smile was precious. "I'd like that."

Together they walked across the campground. Landon's fingers brushed against hers. Much to his surprise, she gently took his hand, weaving her fingers in his. While they'd held hands numerous times, it was usually when there were crowds around or when she was frightened.

Landon knew she took his hand so she could feel safe. But tonight, her touch seemed different. *Could it be Elise's feelings are finally on the same page as mine?*

Side by side, they descended the sloping metal bridge from the campground, entering the rear of the park by the pavilions and Pioneer Train terminal. While fewer than earlier, many people were still in the park. Because they'd already eaten, the scent of grilled meat and popcorn wasn't as appealing as normal.

Landon led Elise to the Scenic Skyway ride. Only a few patrons were ahead of them.

"What kind of ride is this?"

"According to Beth, this was an actual ski lift before they brought it here. I've been told the view from the top is breathtaking." He felt a slight tremble where her hand touched his. "You okay?"

"The mountain is pretty steep."

"Hey, if you're scared of heights, we don't have to do this."

"Heights don't concern me. After all, I wasn't scared of the Ferris Wheel. It's just I've never gone up a mountain that way. Is it safe?"

He touched her face. "Of course, but let's forget it. I'll buy you an ice cream instead."

"I don't mind doing new things... as long as you're there with me."

When their turn came, they quickly sat down. After the safety bar was lowered, Landon placed his feet on the supports. He couldn't help but smile as Elise squeezed his hand.

He was caught off guard when she spoke. "I wanted to thank you for this summer."

"It's been my pleasure."

"Mine as well. I know you've gone out of your way to introduce me to new things. To take me to new places. I never dreamed I'd find someone like you." She leaned back to face him. "Thank you for being my best friend."

He wanted to kiss her so badly, but Landon's desire was to make that first embrace memorable. He could barely wait for the ride to reach the summit and display a breathtaking view of the park. The colorful lights of the rides were beginning to come on as they entered the ride.

"I agree. You are my best friend... well, actually more." He brushed the hair from her eyes. "You're my soulmate, Elise. The greatest joy in my life is spending time with you."

Elise didn't answer, but stared into his eyes. There was a glimpse of something new in her expression Landon hadn't seen before. *Could that be love?*

The trance was broken when their car reached the top and spun around. Suddenly, the iridescent glow from the park twinkled in the twilight below them. A little farther in the distance, a smoky haze hung over the trees hiding the campground. Above them, the first stars were beginning their nightly display. The world was perfect. Landon could wait no longer.

Elise's attention was focused on the panorama before them. He gently touched her chin and turned her to face him. He swallowed hard before beginning.

"Elise, I've never felt like you make me feel. It's like I'm alive when you're with me. I know God meant for us to be together. And I have a confession."

The girl's smile had never been as broad.

"I love you."

Landon leaned forward and found her lips. Much to his surprise, Elise shoved him away and slid across the seat as far away from him as she could.

"What's wrong? Don't you feel the same way?"

"Don't you ever do that again!"

"What? Why?"

Elise was looking away from him and paused before answering. "I don't want this."

If he hadn't been secured in his seat by the safety bar, Landon might have tumbled out. "I don't understand."

"I wanted a best friend, not a boyfriend."

Chapter Nine

Coffee and Revelations

Weeks had passed since the trip to Elysburg. While the days might be hot, most evenings were now chilly. Elise and Landon still hung out together, but not nearly as often. Landon seemed to be depressed and Elise could guess why. She knew she'd hurt him, but didn't know how to make it right. From watching television, she'd observed that couples who fell in love usually didn't stay together, and those who did didn't remain best friends. Elise couldn't risk their friendship.

Elise was restocking the shelves when the shop door opened.

Landon smiled at her. "Hi, Elise. Missed going for a walk with you this morning."

"I was making a pot of chili."

Before she could decide if she wanted to ask if he'd like to join her for dinner, Beth appeared. "Hey,

Landon. I see you have another load of pumpkins and gourds. Are they for us?"

"If you want any of them."

"Sure. I'll take them all. Just put the boxes out front. Elise and I will arrange them later."

Not very long ago, the man would have waited for Elise's help. Together, they would have shared laughter while they worked. But this morning, Landon simply walked outside and removed the items from the truck bed. By himself.

When finished, he brought in paperwork. Turning from Beth, he nodded at Elise. "Hope you have a good day. See ya." Not even waiting for a response, the man departed.

As she watched him drive away, Elise could feel Beth's eyes on her. "Trouble in paradise?"

Elise directed her attention back to the shelves. "I don't know what you mean."

"Uh-huh. Elise, I'm more than your boss. I'm your friend. And I know that ever since Knoebels, something's been off with the two of you. Care to talk about it?"

Elise paused before she responded. "I think I upset Landon."

"Why would you think that?"

"He kissed me on the skyride."

Beth clapped, a smile gracing her face. "Finally. I was wondering when that would happen. I'm happy for you."

"You shouldn't be. I certainly didn't want him to do that."

Beth moved so they were looking at each other. The other woman's face softened. "How about I make us some coffee so we can chat?"

"Okay."

After they were situated, Beth sought her eyes. "Why didn't you want him to kiss you?"

"I just, just, well... I never expected him to do that. After all, he's my best friend. And I don't want to lose that. Best friends don't kiss each other."

"Sometimes they do. After all, my husband Andy is my best friend."

"Wait. I thought you and Selena were best friends."

Beth laughed. "We are, but there's a gigantic difference in my relationship with Selena than the one I have with my husband. Andy and I share our lives with a romantic intimacy I could never have with anyone else. It's as if we are one. Andy completes me. I know you're not a believer, but I am. I trust with my whole heart that God created that man just for me."

"Wait. How can he be your best friend and your husband at the same time?"

"It's simple. God intended for a man and a woman to be together, to share a life and make something special. In the Bible, God says 'a man shall leave his father and mother and hold fast to his wife, and they shall become one flesh'." Beth patted Elise's hand. "What that means is they complement each other in such a way that together, they are greater than they are separately."

Elise stared at her for a while. "But is it really like that? You'll have to understand. I know I'm at a disadvantage because of my childhood isolation, but I'm scared. All my life I dreamed I'd find a best friend like Landon used to be. And because of that stupid kiss, it's all falling apart. What he and I had was all I ever wanted. Why couldn't things have stayed the way they were?"

"Has he treated you differently since then? Was Landon upset that you rejected him?"

"N-no, not really. I think it's more like I hurt him. We were so close and now our friendship is like it was when we first met. It's awkward."

Beth took a sip of her coffee. "And how do you feel about Landon?"

The man's face flashed before her. "Beth, he really is my best friend. I've never been happier in life than when I'm with him. That is, before this happened."

"The happiness part, that's a good thing."

"But I'm afraid of change. I kind of see what you're saying, but suppose this whole kiss thing goes wrong and drives us apart? That's what always happens on TV."

After a long silence, Beth added, "That is a possibility, but what if it draws you even closer? Let's face it, Elise. That man loves you and has for a long while. I'm not the only one who sees it—Selena agrees as well. Perhaps it's time the two of you *really* talked this out. I have the feeling you might be pleasantly surprised."

"But I don't even know what love is."

"I can help with that." Beth stood and walked into her office. She returned with a book. "This is the Bible, God's word. I've opened it to First

Corinthians, chapter thirteen. It was a letter Paul sent to the people of Corinth. If you really want to know what true love is, look at verses four through eight. I've got to tell you, before you two had your falling out, this is exactly how I saw the two of you."

For the rest of her shift, Elise pondered the words she had read. Could it really be that Landon did truly love her? And that he could be not only her best friend, but something more?

Glad she had driven to work instead of walking, Elise pointed her car in the direction of Landon's farm. She had decided to invite him over for dinner. Beth was right. Elise and Landon had a lot to talk about.

It seemed to take forever, but his homestead finally came into view. Elise depressed the turn signal, but stopped at the end of the lane.

Landon was in the pasture, walking along the fence. There was a woman with him. In utter disbelief, she watched as the two embraced.

Elise quickly drove off before Landon even knew she was there.

Chapter Ten

Behind the Curtain

Somehow, Elise managed to drive back home, but she was so full of disappointment that she couldn't walk inside.

Still parked in the drive, Elise opened the book Beth had given her. Quickly finding the page she'd studied earlier, she read the passage again.

Love never gives up. Thinking back, there were many times when things were difficult between them, but Landon stuck with her. He never gave up and always had a smile.

Love cares more for others than for self. The man had bent over backwards to show her the world around her, making sure that Elise felt safe. He was so gentle and kind, always taking her thoughts and concerns into consideration prior to taking action.

Love doesn't want what it doesn't have. It doesn't force itself, isn't always me first. It puts up with anything, always looks for the best. It keeps going until the end.

Hand over her mouth, she closed the book. "Beth was right. That was us. These words were written for me to read."

Elise had difficulty breathing. It felt like a curtain had been drawn back and she saw the world in a new light, as if for the first time. "Landon really does love me." Then the memory of him hugging that other woman jumped into her mind. "Yet, if he truly loved me, why would he be with her? Did Landon stop loving me?" If he did indeed quit loving Elise, had it even been love in the first place?

Suddenly, a warm calmness wrapped itself around her, slowly filling her mind and heart. A sudden desire to again see these words God had supposedly written moved her to pick up the Bible.

Grasping it by the covers, the pages split by themselves and Elise was once again looking at First Corinthians, chapter thirteen. But there was something different. Three little words stuck out, as if they were highlighted by a light a thousand times brighter than the sun.

She read them, over and over again. And in that instant, she knew God was there, and He was speaking directly to her.

Love never dies.

***

"I'm impressed with what you've done with the place. Your mom and dad would be proud of you."

Landon smiled. "Thanks, Quinn. Dad might think my herd of Black Angus is a little sparse, but wouldn't Mom be happy? I took twenty acres of produce to market this year."

The short-haired lady nodded. "I believe you inherited her green thumb." Quinn pulled her sweater tightly around her shoulders. "Do you think it's chilly in here or is it my imagination?"

Walking over to the thermostat, Landon noted the room temperature was less than the set point. "I'll walk downstairs and check the heater. I've been having problems with that old boiler starting up."

He had just re-ignited the pilot light when a loud knock resonated from the floor above. Before he could climb the stairs, Landon heard Quinn open the door.

A smile crossed his face as he listened to Quinn ask, "May I help you? Oh wait, are you Elise? Landon told me so much about you that I feel I know you."

"Well, I don't know you. I need to see Landon, *now*." There seemed to be anger, or was it urgency, in the girl's voice?

"Please come in."

"Thank you, but I prefer to wait outside. Please send Landon out." The front door closed.

He had just stepped into the kitchen when Quinn called out to him. "You have a visitor. I think it's your friend." The lady touched his hand and smiled. "And you're right. She is very pretty."

"I agree. I'll be back in soon."

He stepped out into the chilly night air. Elise was sitting on the porch steps facing away from the door.

He stepped onto the walkway and turned so they were face to face. "Hey. It's nice to see you. What's up?"

Her expression was different, as if she were suddenly confident. "I get it now."

"What do you mean?"

"Everything you've been telling and showing me for the last couple of months. I know it's real."

"I don't understand, Elise."

"Ever since we met, there were two things you've been sharing with me. And tonight, my eyes are open. I finally comprehend it... on both accounts." Even with the dimness of the evening, Landon couldn't miss it. Elise had a glow about her, especially her eyes.

"Tell me what you mean."

"You took your time. You never forced it. And you've been waiting for me, haven't you?"

Joy seemed to well up from within. "I guess that depends on what you're talking about."

"The first is God. You knew I didn't believe, but you do. You never forced it down my throat. It all came back tonight. I recalled every conversation we had—about how a maple leaf was made, or the order of the stars hung in the skies. That was your way of gently introducing me to Him."

"I really hoped you would eventually believe, but I wanted you to make that decision. I would never force you."

She nodded and looked away for a moment. Elise's words were whisper quiet, as if she were speaking to herself. *"It never wants its own way."*

"What did you say?"

Elise stood and took his hands. "Love never wants its own way. Today was the first time I ever read the Bible. Beth gave me hers. Do you know what I read?"

"No."

"I read about love. What true love is. How God meant it to be."

He squeezed her hands. "You read first Corinthians, chapter thirteen, didn't you?"

Elise nodded. "And do you know what I found?"

"What's that?"

She sniffed and released his hands. Hers were trembling when she touched his face, pulling his toward hers. "I found you."

Elise kissed him softly, then wrapped her arms tightly around him.

"I love you, Landon. It just took me a while to figure it out."

Joy! Happiness! Mirth! He'd never before experienced this. *Thank You, God.* "I love you, too."

She pulled away until their eyes met. "But there's one thing I need you to do."

"What's that?"

"Don't give up on me. I need my best friend. Please, get rid of that girl, right now. Send her away."

"Oh Elise, I will always be your best friend. But why do you want Quinn to leave?"

"Because I saw you hugging her earlier. I, I just..."

Landon couldn't control his laughter. "Come in. Let me introduce you."

"But I don't want anyone to come between us."

He couldn't resist and kissed her again. "I promise you, nothing ever will. Let's go inside where it's warm."

Elise followed him until they were standing in the vestibule. The other woman stood and smiled when they entered.

"Quinn," Landon motioned from one to the other of them. "I'd like to introduce you to my best friend, Elise."

The lady smiled and extended her hand. "It's a pleasure to finally meet you."

He could tell it took an effort for Elise to shake the woman's hand. "Hi."

Now Landon looked directly into Elise's eyes. "And Elise, I'd like to introduce you to Quinn White... my cousin."

Chapter Eleven

That Enchanted Evening

They stood outside Beth and Andy Warren's house. Elise's head was spinning. She and Landon had danced to every song. Beth and her friend Selena had hosted the reception after Elise and Landon's wedding at Landon's—no, scratch that, *their* farm. And God's presence had been everywhere. He had even decorated the trees with red, yellow and orange leaves to provide a beautiful background for their celebration.

"You two look so happy." Beth's expression was one of delight.

Elise squeezed her husband's hand. "Today is the happiest day of my life."

"I think she had too much champagne," Selena managed to say with a straight face.

"I'm driving, so quit picking on my bride." Landon touched Elise's cheek. "And so you know, today's the best day of my life as well." He pressed his lips to her forehead. "That's because I'm the luckiest man in the world. God sent me the woman I've prayed for... to be my soulmate forever."

Selena shook her head as she laughed. "Tell me again, where are you going for your honeymoon?"

"We should be thanked for the honeymoon accommodations." Everyone turned to find Terry Faughtinger and her husband AJ standing there. "Isn't that right?" The writer elbowed her spouse.

"Honey, stop it. I want my sister and her husband to enjoy themselves. So don't worry about the animals. We'll take care of them."

"Uh, you might." Terry held up her hands. "These babies were made for conjuring up horror scenes, not cleaning after cows that aren't house broken."

"I think you mean barn broken, if there was such a thing. But I bet if you read them one of your books, they'd race outside to get away from you."

"And this is why we're going away. Let's answer Selena before we go." Landon nodded slightly.

Elise picked up on the silent message. Her *husband* wanted her to be the one to answer.

"We're spending tonight in Baltimore," she said, "at a hotel overlooking the harbor. That's where Landon took me on our first date. Tomorrow, we're flying to Florida to catch our cruise ship to Saint Thomas. Giving credit where it's due, Terry gave us the cruise as a wedding present." She turned to take in the beaming smile of the man she loved. "And then? Who cares, as long as we're together. After all, we've got eternity to share."

After goodbyes, they pointed Elise's car in the general direction of Baltimore. Landon was driving, but warmly held her hand. The interior was filled with the scent of the special flowers her man had given her.

His voice interrupted the solitude. "You're quiet. Is everything okay?"

It was better than okay. Today was perfect. "Absolutely. I wanted to share something with you."

"I love it when we share."

"I'm not sure if it was a dream or just my mind wandering, but I thought about our story. As you know, my world was turned upside-down when I found out who I really was—that my name was Elise, not Laura. And that my parents lived here and I had a brother. That the people who raised me weren't my real parents, but instead, they were the ones who had abducted me."

"I'm sorry, sweetie."

"That's okay. Keep listening. They had never mentioned God and after they passed, I scoffed at the possibility He even existed. I mean, where was He the whole time they kept me isolated on that mountain?"

Landon raised her arm to kiss her fingers. "I know this is hard to fathom, but there's a reason for everything."

"Um-hmm. I understand that now. My heart had to be ready for you. You're a great man, Landon. It was your actions that helped me understand that God is real. And then how you helped me explore and understand the Bible—discovering Jesus' love for us. Just think, you and I will live *forever*. That blows me away. You were exactly what I needed, precisely when I needed it. And you, Landon are the perfect blessing God created only for me."

"I prayed for a woman to love, and what did God do? He sent me an angel. I was beginning to think I'd never find anyone... and then, He sends me *the* one."

Elise leaned across and kissed her husband's cheek. "I'm so happy it was me. He was waiting for the time to be right—for you and I to meet. Until you came along, I was walking the lonely road of life by myself. But since I met you, you've always known just what I needed."

"That's because I love you, Mrs. Elise Brianna... no longer Showers, but instead, White. I mean, the day we finally met... I just felt such a connection with you. As if my life changed completely." Her husband had such a dreamy look in his eyes.

"For the good, I hope."

"Absolutely. I will always remember the first day when I stopped by Beth's store and you were there. After I left, I couldn't get you out of my mind. This is gonna sound crazy, but the next morning I went for a walk in the woods behind the farm. I sang all these sappy love songs for you. Silly, I know, but it felt like you were there with me."

Elise laughed so hard, if the seat belt hadn't been there, she would have fallen to the floor. "That's because I was there, silly—you just didn't see me. I had also taken a hike behind the farm that day—hoping I'd catch a glimpse of you. Then I heard this tremendous commotion behind me."

"A commotion? What was it?"

"You, singing. I was hiding in the pines, but heard every word." Elise squeezed his hand extra tight. "And that last song touched me. You were singing *Some Enchanted Evening*. Deep inside, I wished you were serenading me."

Landon laughed. "In my mind, I was. Incidentally, do you know how the musical ends?"

"No, I don't really remember."

"Despite all odds, Emile returns from the war. While it doesn't come out and say it, you just know they are going to spend the rest of their lives together, deeply in love. Kind of like you and me. We made it through our struggles and now a future of happiness is ours."

"Talk about a wish come true. Thank you, for loving me."

Landon pulled to the side of the road and drew Elise into his arms. "I do love you with my whole heart and always will. And that lonely road you mentioned?"

"Yes?"

"Don't worry. From now until the end of eternity, you'll never again walk it alone."

The End

Want to see where it all started?

**If you liked *The Lonely Road*,
you'll love these...**

Treasure in Paradise
While researching characters for her upcoming book, Jasmine finds a real doozy in Josh Miller, a highly talented man who is doing his best to keep his skills hidden. Jasmine knows he's hiding something, so she keeps digging into Josh's life. Who knows? If she mines deep enough, she might find treasure.

Scan this QR code to order *Treasure in Paradise,* Christian Journeys in Paradise, Book 7.

paperback

large print

Road to Paradise
Beth may be young, but she knows what she wants – a once-in-a-lifetime fairytale romance. After her first date with Anderson Warren, she believes she's met Prince Charming. But when his ex-fiancée storms into town like a tornado and leaves a swath

of destruction between them, is there any way to put in back together?

Scan this QR code to order *Road to Paradise,* a Paradise Sweetheart Romance Novella.

Autumn in Paradise

Everything Annie worked for is gone. After losing both her job and boyfriend, she moves to Lancaster to start over. She soon finds herself in the company of two men. One is her mind's perfect choice, yet the other pulls at her heartstrings. Which should she follow – her mind or her heart? Scan this QR code to order *Autumn in Paradise*, Christian Journeys in Paradise, Book 8.

paperback

large print

West of Paradise

After three failed marriages, Teresa believes true love isn't on the menu. Until she meets red-bearded, ex-sea captain AJ Showers. It seems the man's mission is to make her life a wonderful dream. But when Teresa discovers the secret that AJ and the young neighbor woman share, will their romance sink... or will they sail off into the sunset happily ever after?

Scan this QR code to order *West of Paradise,* a Paradise Sweetheart Romance Novella.

South Mountain Series

Destiny

Selena stands at a crossroad in life. Her parents are gone, the man she wanted rejected her and she's been forced out of the job she loved. It's time for a fresh start, but where? On a sunny bench in Maryland, she runs into the man from her past and his new girl. But wait – is this a chance encounter, or the beginning of the path to her true destiny? Scan this QR code to order *Destiny*, South Mountain Journey of Faith, Book 1.

Want to read more of Chas's books?

Get **Skating in Paradise** free
when you subscribe to the newsletter.

Visit www.ChasWilliamson.com
to claim your free book!

Every day is a struggle for oncology nurse Tammy Kunkle. After cancer took both her little girl and husband, she's dedicated her life solely to helping others. But when she visits a former child patient, she's introduced to a man filled with a warm, faithful spirit. Could it be Tammy has met her future?

Download your free copy of
Skating in Paradise today.

www.chaswilliamson.com

Did you like *The Lonely Road*?
Please consider leaving a review for other readers.

For a complete list of Chas's books visit
www.ChasWilliamson.com

Dedication

To Janet

The Lonely Road is a story of discovery. For our heroine, a world she never knew is waiting for her.

This book is dedicated to the woman who helped me discover not only the world, but my future. You helped me find true love and happiness. You worked unceasingly to help me achieve my dreams.

And just like Landon did for Elise, you showed me what love really is, not just in words, but by actions.

I shudder to think what I would have become, if not for you. God sent you to direct my footsteps, to encourage me when I failed, to offer your hand when I stumbled. You showed me not only love, but how to love. I am who I am because of you.

In my eyes, you are truly an angel and this book, and my life, are forever dedicated to you, Janet.

True love lasts forever!

Acknowledgments

To God, for the gift of his Son to give us salvation and everlasting life.

To Janet, my favorite person. You are the light of my life, my inspiration, my joy, my world, my eternal destiny.

To Demi, editor, publisher and friend. Thank you for helping me change from being a writer to an author.

To the team of Janet, Sarah, Connie, Mary, and Diane for their assistance and guidance as we now journey farther along *South Mountain*.

To my children and grandchildren. These books are the legacy of love I leave for you.

To the three who are our future. Never allow peer pressure and temptation to lead you astray. You have a purpose, a destiny. May you always do what is right and boldly follow your heart. Don't be afraid to leave a trail of love others will follow. Remember Mimi and I believe in you. We will always be with you, in your heart if not by your side.

To my fans. My wish is that God uses the words He placed in my heart to bless your lives. Thank you for being a fan!

To the angels who walk among us. Like them, we should strive to pass on the love and grace that God has given to us.

About the Author

Chas Williamson's lifelong dream was to write. He started writing his first book at age eight, but quit after two paragraphs. Yet some dreams never fade...

It's said one should write what one knows best. That left two choices—the world of environmental health and safety... or romance. Chas and his bride have built a fairytale life of love. At her encouragement, he began writing romance. The characters you'll meet in his books are very real to him, and he hopes they'll become just as real to you.

True Love Lasts Forever!

Follow Chas on www.bookbub.com

 Check out our website at
ChasWilliamson.com

 Check us out on Facebook at
Chas Williamson Books

 Follow us on Instagram at
Chas Williamson

Made in the USA
Middletown, DE
03 July 2023